RAINBOW
magic®
The Sporty Fairies

For all the children of
Newbridge Primary School

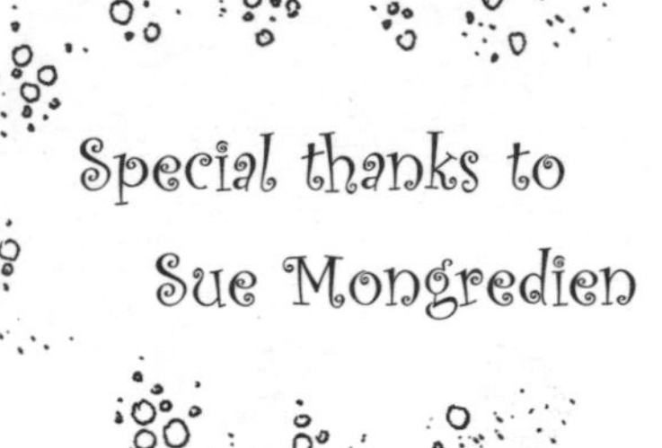

Special thanks to
Sue Mongredien

ORCHARD BOOKS
338 Euston Road, London NW1 3BH
Orchard Books Australia
Level 17/207 Kent Street, Sydney, NSW 2000
A Paperback Original

First published in 2008 by Orchard Books.

A CIP catalogue record for this book is available
from the British Library.

ISBN 978 1 84616 892 5
14

Printed in Great Britain

Orchard Books is a division of Hachette Children's Books,
an Hachette UK company

www.hachette.co.uk

Samantha the Swimming Fairy

by Daisy Meadows

ORCHARD

The Fairyland Palace
Fairyla
Car Park
Coaches
Cooke Football Stadium
Riding Stables
Netball Courts
Tippington Town
Football Pitches
LEISURE CENTRE
Swimming Pool

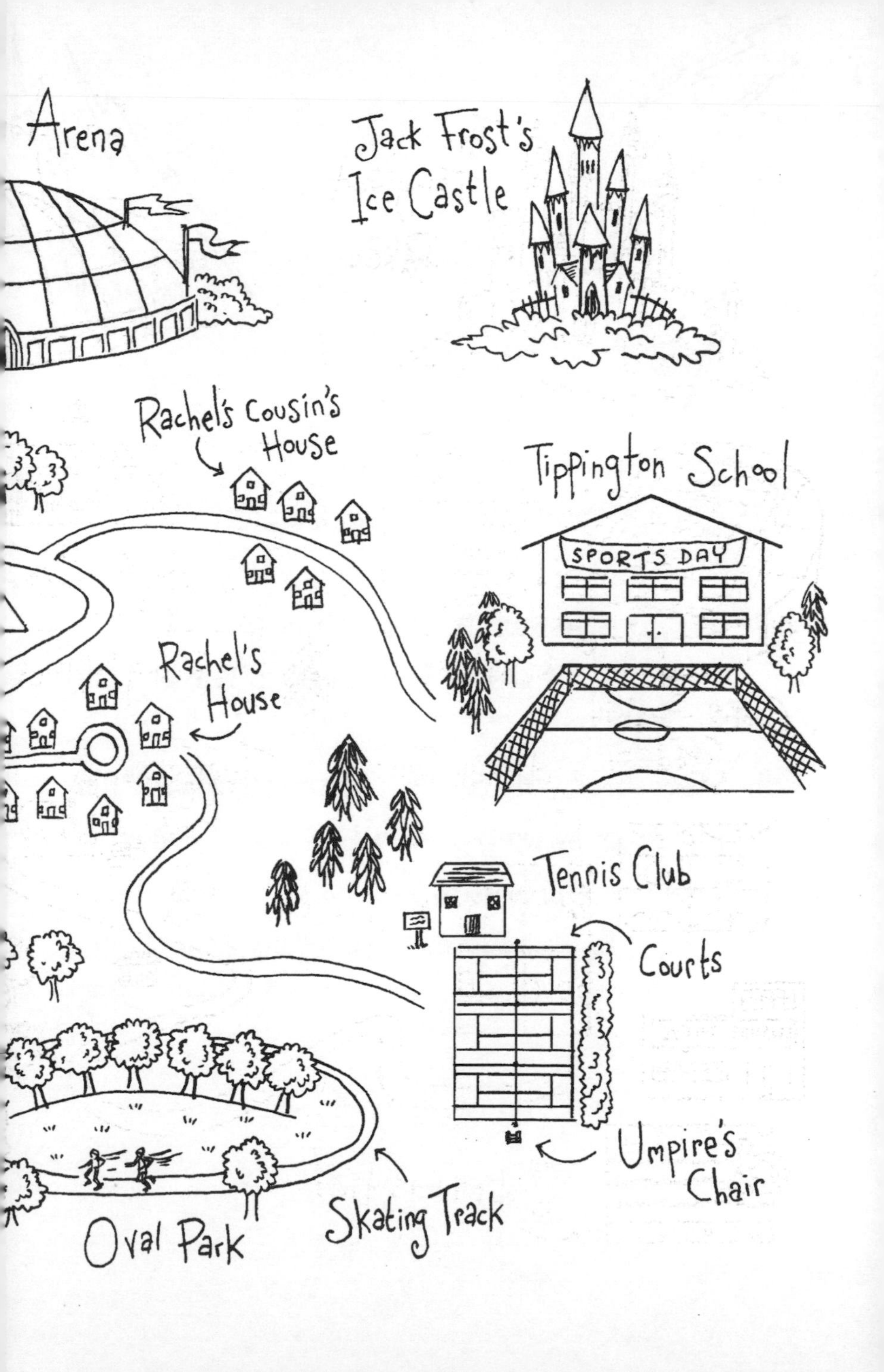
Arena
Jack Frost's Ice Castle
Rachel's Cousin's House
Tippington School
SPORTS DAY
Rachel's House
Tennis Club
Courts
Umpire's Chair
Skating Track
Oval Park

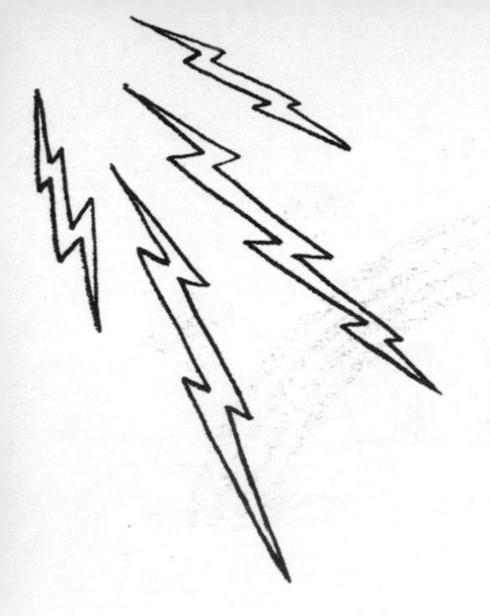

The Fairyland Olympics are about to start,
And my crafty goblins are going to take part.
We'll win this year, for I've got a cunning plan.
I'm sending my goblins to the arena in Fairyland.

The Magic Sporty Objects that make sports safe and fun,
Will be stolen by my goblins, to keep until we've won.
Sporty Fairies, prepare to lose and to watch us win.
Goblins, follow my commands, and let the games begin!

Contents

"Fetch, Buttons!" Rachel Walker called, throwing her dog's favourite ball down the garden.

Kirsty Tate, Rachel's best friend, who was staying with the Walkers for a week of the Easter holidays, smiled. "Buttons loves exercise, doesn't he?" she said, as the dog bounded after the ball.

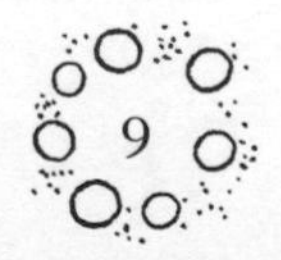

"And we're nearly as fit as him, after the sporty week we've had so far!"

Rachel grinned. Unknown to her parents, she and Kirsty had been on a new fairy adventure this week, helping the Sporty Fairies track down their missing Magic Sporty Objects. Rachel felt as if she and Kirsty were the luckiest girls in the world, being friends with the fairies.

"Good dog!" said Rachel's dad, coming out into the garden with Mrs Walker, as Buttons rushed back with the ball in his mouth. Buttons dropped the ball at Rachel's feet, then went to his water bowl to drink thirstily.

"Phew, it's hot," Mrs Walker said, fanning herself. "The perfect day for a swim, I'd say."

Rachel and Kirsty looked at one another excitedly. Swimming would be a great idea – especially as Samantha the Swimming Fairy's Magic Goggles were still missing.

"Ooh, yes, can we go swimming?" Rachel asked.

"Tippington Pool is closed," Mr Walker pointed out, "so you'd have to go to Aqua World in the next village." Then he frowned. "But the car's being serviced in the garage; I won't be able to drive you there."

Kirsty felt disappointed, as she loved swimming. At the start of the week, she and Rachel had discovered that naughty Jack Frost had sent his goblins to steal the Sporty Fairies' Magic Sporty Objects. When the objects were with the Sporty Fairies – or in their lockers in the Fairyland Arena – they made sure that sports in the human world and in Fairyland were safe, fun and played fairly. But, when they weren't in place, sports everywhere were ruined and disrupted and only those people very close to a Magic Sporty Object were good at that particular sport.

The Fairyland Olympics were due to be held soon and Jack Frost wanted his goblins to use the objects' powers to cheat in the contest and win the big prize – a golden cup full of luck. Kirsty and Rachel knew that the goblins were practising hard for their events, so the goblins with Samantha's Magic Goggles were sure to be found in a swimming pool somewhere.

"You could get the bus," Mrs Walker said. "The 41 goes all the way there. If you take your mobile, Rachel, you can let me know when you'll be back."

"Yay!" cheered Rachel and Kirsty together. They both dashed inside to pack their swimming things, then Rachel's mum walked them to the bus stop.

They didn't have to wait long before a bus pulled up. The girls waved goodbye to Mrs Walker and sat together at the back of the bus where the seats were slightly higher and they had a good view out of the window.

Kirsty gazed out at the houses and the bus set off.

As they waited at some traffic lights, Kirsty noticed that they had stopped near Tippington Swimming Pool. A sign outside read 'CLOSED FOR MAINTENANCE'. The building had a glass front, tinted at the bottom to prevent people looking in, but clear at the top.

A huge pipe wrapped around the outside of the building. Kirsty guessed it must be a water slide.

Suddenly, Kirsty noticed a flash of green pop up above the level of the tinted glass. She blinked and stared. What was that?

The green thing appeared again and Kirsty let out a gasp. She was sure she'd just seen a goblin!

Goblins Galore!

Kirsty nudged Rachel. "Look!" she hissed, pointing.

As the girls watched, the goblin popped up again and Rachel's eyes shone excitedly. "How lucky that you spotted him!" she exclaimed. "If he's in there, I bet Samantha's Magic Goggles are, too."

"But why does he keep popping up and

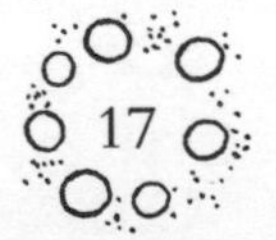

then vanishing?" Kirsty wondered, as the goblin appeared above the tinted glass once more.

"He must be bouncing on the diving board," Rachel giggled. She stood up and pressed the bell to tell the driver that they wanted to get off. "Come on," she said, "let's investigate. We can go to Aqua World afterwards."

Kirsty jumped up eagerly. Another fairy adventure was beginning!

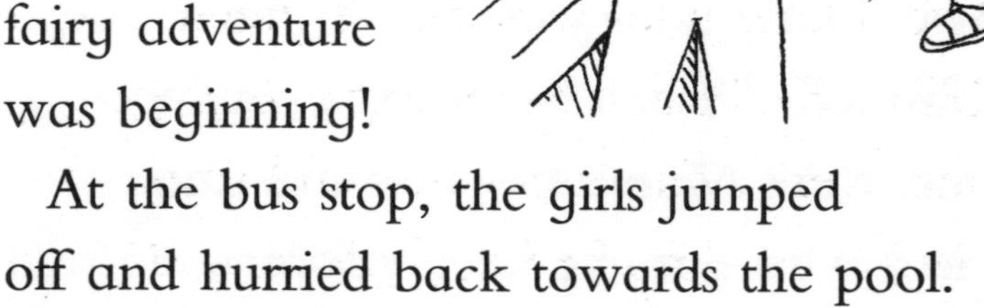

At the bus stop, the girls jumped off and hurried back towards the pool.

"I didn't notice the goblin wearing any goggles," Kirsty said.

"Nor me," Rachel agreed. "But maybe there are two of them in there."

Kirsty and Rachel went round to the side of the building and pressed their faces up against the glass so that they could see in more clearly. Then they both gasped in amazement.

"There are goblins everywhere!" Rachel cried.

The whole pool was full of green goblins of all sizes. Some were diving, others were swimming laps and some were just playing in the shallow end.

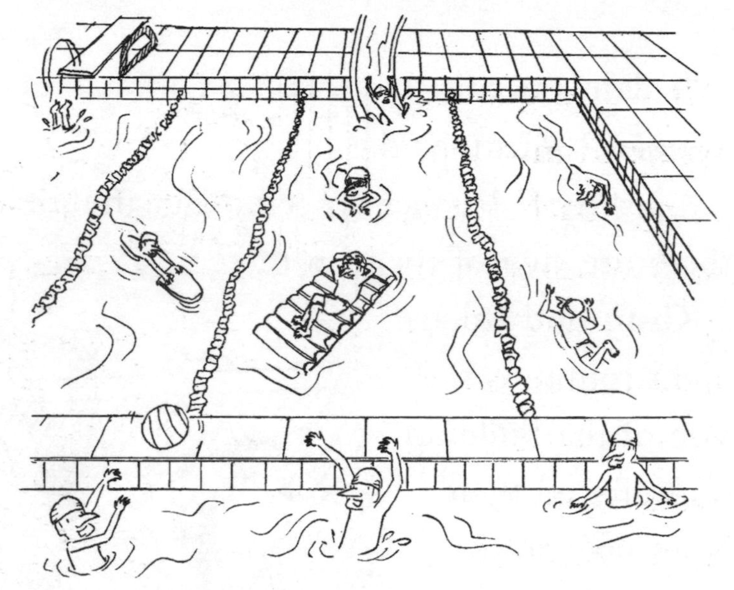

"We'd better get in there, and start looking for the Magic Goggles," Kirsty said. "It might take us a while."

The girls crept along, looking for a way inside the building. Unfortunately, the whole place seemed securely locked up. Then Rachel heard footsteps and the girls darted behind a bush. They peeped through the leaves, and saw a figure coming towards them.

It was a goblin, wrapped in a big, stripy beach towel, and wearing a white swimming hat and red goggles on his head!

"Are those Samantha's Magic Goggles?" Rachel asked Kirsty in a whisper.

Kirsty shook her head. "I think those are just ordinary ones," she whispered back. "They don't look magical. The other Magic Sporty Objects have all sparkled with fairy magic."

The girls watched as the goblin walked to a nearby tree, and climbed up into its branches. Then he started crawling along a thick branch that led all the way to an open window in the building. The goblin reached the window and wriggled through it, disappearing from view.

"So that's how they've been getting in," Kirsty said. "Let's try it."

She and Rachel climbed up the tree, along the branch and in through the window, just as the goblin had done. They found themselves in a tiled corridor.

"I know where we are," Rachel said confidently. "The pools are this way."

She led Kirsty down the corridor. Faint shouts and squeals of excitement echoed up from the pools, and the girls crept along cautiously, not wanting to be seen.

At the end, they peeped around the corner. Kirsty saw two pools, a large one with a water slide at the back, and a smaller, shallower pool in front. In the small pool, seven goblins, all wearing nose clips, floated on the surface. They lay with their heads together in the middle of the pool, while their legs pointed out to the sides. It reminded Kirsty of a wheel, with goblins for spokes.

"What are they doing?" she murmured.

Rachel tried not to laugh out loud. "They're practising synchronised swimming!" she hissed. "I can't see any sparkly shimmers on their goggles though, can you?"

The girls peered carefully at all the goggles on the goblins' heads, but they all seemed quite ordinary.

Then the goblins flipped over into handstands, with their bodies underwater and their legs sticking out, toes pointed. They each lowered their left legs, and turned in the water at the same time.

"Come on, let's get past them while they're underwater," Kirsty said. "Then we can search the main pool."

The girls raced past the small pool, and hid behind a pile of lilos. Then Rachel noticed something interesting ahead. She nudged Kirsty. "Do you see those floats over there?"

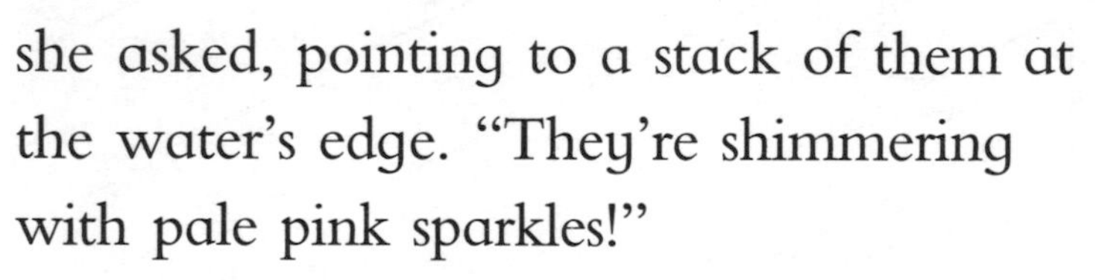

she asked, pointing to a stack of them at the water's edge. "They're shimmering with pale pink sparkles!"

"Maybe the Magic Goggles have been left there," Kirsty whispered. "Let's go and check."

The two friends ran over for a closer look. There was no sign of the Magic Goggles,

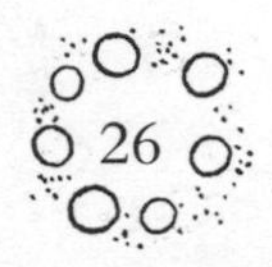

but both girls smiled when they saw what was causing the sparkles. Perched on the top of the pile of floats, her tiny legs dangling over the edge, was Samantha the Swimming Fairy!

Samantha had long dark hair, and a pink and black swimming costume, with a pretty pink sarong-style skirt. "Hello there, girls!" she said cheerfully.

"Hello," Rachel smiled. "We're on the hunt for your Magic Goggles!"

"Me too," Samantha said. "I can sense that they're in this building."

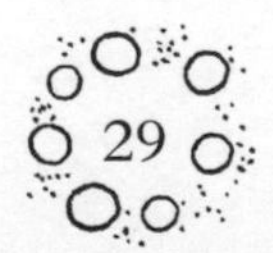

She grinned at the girls. "But I can't let you stay in those jeans and T-shirts! Let's get you something more suitable to wear..." She waved her wand and a stream of glittering, powder-pink fairy dust swirled from its tip, tumbling around the girls. Seconds later, their clothes were replaced with two-piece swim-skirt suits. Rachel's was lilac with a silvery dolphin pattern on it, and Kirsty's was turquoise with a gold seashell print.

"That's more like it!" smiled Samantha.

"Ooh, thank you," Kirsty said, admiring her costume. "Now we should try looking in the big pool for your goggles, Samantha. None of the goblins in the little pool have them."

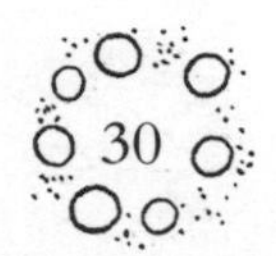

Rachel pointed to the spectators' seats that ran along the side of the main pool. "Let's nip behind those," she suggested. "Then we can peep out to look for the goggles but stay hidden."

"Good idea," Samantha agreed.

Together, the two girls and their fairy friend crept behind the plastic seating, and peered out between the chairs.

Kirsty noticed a goblin wearing a T-shirt that said LIFEGUARD on the front. He was sitting up in a high chair by the side of the pool and shouting instructions to the other goblins. But Kirsty's eye was caught by what dangled from his left hand – a pair of sparkling pink goggles! "Over there," she whispered excitedly to her friends. "I think it's the Magic Goggles!"

Samantha beamed. "Yes, it is!" she cheered quietly. "Well spotted!"

"Now we just need to think of a way to get hold of them," Rachel said thoughtfully.

"Why don't I turn you two into fairies?" Samantha suggested. "That way we can try to fly really close to the lifeguard without him noticing – and, with a bit of luck, sneak the goggles straight out of his hand."

Rachel and Kirsty nodded.

"Yes, let's try it," Kirsty said eagerly.

Samantha waved her wand, and, once more, a cloud of light pink sparkles spun around the girls. This time they felt themselves shrinking down and down until they were fairy-sized.

It's always so exciting, turning into a fairy! thought Kirsty. She fluttered her wings happily, loving the way they shone with all the colours of the rainbow under the bright lights above the pool.

"Let's go goggle-grabbing," Rachel giggled as she zoomed into the air. Kirsty and Samantha followed, keeping as close to the ceiling as they could so that the goblins in the pool wouldn't notice them.

As they got closer to the lifeguard, Rachel could hear him bragging.

"I'm the lifeguard, that means I'm in charge," he was telling some other goblins. "And I say no splashing, no cannon-balling and no dunking!"

"We're only having a bit of fun," a small goblin replied. "You're a meanie!"

"Rules are rules!" retorted the lifeguard. He pointed to his T-shirt in a self-important manner. "Read the T-shirt!" he ordered. "I'm the lifeguard – what I say goes!"

Kirsty, Rachel and Samantha hovered behind the lifeguard's chair, waiting for a good moment to grab the goggles. But the lifeguard kept a tight hold of them, swinging them from his finger and thumb.

Now a different goblin with a cheeky expression approached. "It's my turn to have those," he said, pointing to the Magic Goggles. "You've had them for ages, and you're not even using them! I want to wear them on the water slide."

"Certainly not," the lifeguard sniffed. "Water-sliding is not an Olympic sport! We've come here to practise Olympic water events, remember, not to mess about on slides."

"But—" the other goblin began.

But the lifeguard was in full flow now. "Have you forgotten that the Fairyland Olympics is only two days away?" he continued. "Two days! That's all you've got! So practise your lengths instead of sliding, please. Jack Frost won't be very happy if he hears about this."

The other goblin stomped off in a huff, and Kirsty thought the lifeguard goblin looked rather smug as he watched him go. He twirled the Magic Goggles around one of his knobbly fingers.

The three fairies exchanged glances and flew a little nearer, hoping to slip the goggles off the lifeguard's finger and zoom away with them. But, just then, there came a cry of alarm from the water.

"Help!"

Kirsty, Rachel and Samantha all turned to see what was happening. A goblin was flailing around in the

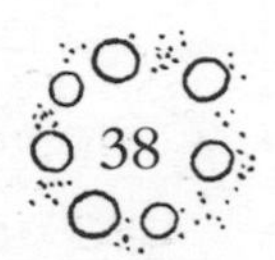

deep end at the opposite side of the pool, thrashing his arms and splashing water everywhere. “Help!” he spluttered again, and then slipped below the surface.

The lifeguard immediately put the Magic Goggles on and dived into the water with a huge splash.

The three fairies watched as he powered across the pool, his long green arms scooping the water in a perfect front crawl. In just a few strong strokes, he'd reached the struggling goblin and

was towing him to safety. He popped the Magic Goggles on top of his head as he reached the side of the pool.

"Wow!" Rachel said admiringly. "What a brilliant swimmer – or, rather, your goggles are brilliant, Samantha, for making him swim so well."

Samantha nodded. "They are very powerful goggles," she agreed proudly. Then her eyes widened. "What's happening over there?"

Kirsty and Rachel looked and saw that the goblin who'd asked to borrow the Magic Goggles was now swimming up behind the lifeguard goblin. Suddenly, he stretched out his arm and swiped the Magic Goggles from the top of the lifeguard's head. Then he swam off with them towards the water slide.

"He is *so* cheeky!" Rachel exclaimed.

"The lifeguard didn't notice a thing," Kirsty added, watching as the lifeguard pulled the struggling goblin out of the water and onto the poolside.

The rescued goblin spluttered and coughed. "I thought I was going blind!" he wailed dramatically.

"Blind? Why?" the lifeguard asked.

The rescued goblin coughed again. "I got water in my eyes and it stung," he explained.

"Ahh," the lifeguard said, wagging a finger. "If you want to keep water out of your eyes, you need a pair of goggles like mine."

The rescued goblin frowned. "But you're not wearing any goggles," he replied, sounding confused.

The lifeguard clicked his tongue in an impatient sort of way. "Well, I keep them up here when I'm not actually swimming," he explained, pointing a finger at the top of his head, where the Magic Goggles had been just seconds earlier.

"Up where? I can't see them!" the rescued goblin said, completely bewildered now.

The lifeguard rolled his eyes. "Then you need glasses, not goggles!" he snapped. "Or maybe a new brain," he muttered. "Honestly!"

Samantha, Kirsty and Rachel couldn't help laughing.

"Come on, that rescued goblin's fine. Let's find the cheeky goblin who took my goggles," Samantha said.

The three friends flew across the pool, looking out for the tell-tale shimmer of the Magic Goggles. The water was still full of goblins, but after a minute or so, Kirsty caught a glimpse of pink sparkles and pointed them out to her friends.

"There!" she said. "He's swimming in the deep end, do you see?"

Rachel and Samantha both watched. The goblin with the goggles was slicing through the water with a very impressive front crawl, wearing the goggles as he swam.

The three friends zoomed after the goblin but he was going very fast. Before they'd had a chance to catch up, he'd reached the other end of the pool and the entrance to the water slide. He got out, pushing the goggles

onto his head. Then he rushed up the steps to the slide, barging through a whole crowd of other goblins who were waiting their turn. "Let me past! Get out of the way!" he shouted. "Goblin with goggles coming through!"

It wasn't long before a scuffle broke out among the goblins at the top of the slide.

"Stop pushing!" shouted one.

"Wait your turn!" cried another.

"You're treading on my toes!" yelped somebody else.

Kirsty, Rachel and Samantha looked at one another despairingly. How were they going to get the goggles back now that they were so tightly surrounded by goblins?

Spotted!

Rachel racked her brains, but it was hard to concentrate because a noisy argument was taking place between two goblins in the pool down below.

"It's my turn for the rubber ring," said the taller of the goblins, trying to snatch it from the other's hands.

"No way! I only just got it!" the

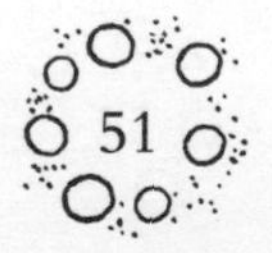

second goblin snapped. "It won't fit you anyway. It's too small for you."

The tall goblin looked offended and splashed the second goblin in the face before swimming away angrily.

But their squabble had given Rachel an idea. "Samantha, would you be able to magic up an inflatable ring?" she asked.

"Of course," said Samantha, holding out her wand.

"And could you make it slightly smaller than usual, please?" Rachel went on.

Samantha nodded. "No problem," she replied. "Why?"

"Well," Rachel began, "I was thinking that we could hold it at the end of the water slide. Then, when the goblin with the Magic Goggles comes shooting out of the slide, he'll go straight into the rubber ring, and if the rubber ring's a little tight, it might trap his arms by his sides."

Kirsty grinned. "And then we'll be able to take the Magic Goggles right off his head!" she finished. "Brilliant, Rachel!"

Samantha was smiling. "I love it," she agreed. "And I can use my fairy magic to make the ring just the right size to pin the goblin's arms to his sides without hurting him. Let's see..." She muttered some magical words and waved her wand. Bright pink fairy dust shot from the end of it, and then a tiny turquoise rubber ring appeared from nowhere, hovering in mid-air.

Rachel beamed. "Perfect," she said, flying to take hold of it.

"I made it tiny for now, so we can carry it easily and it won't be spotted by the goblins," Samantha said. "I'll magic it bigger when the time comes to use it. Let's take it over to the end of the slide and wait for our goblin."

The three of them carried the rubber ring through the air and hovered near the exit to the water slide. Lots of goblins were shooting down the slide, one after another, and splashing into the pool.

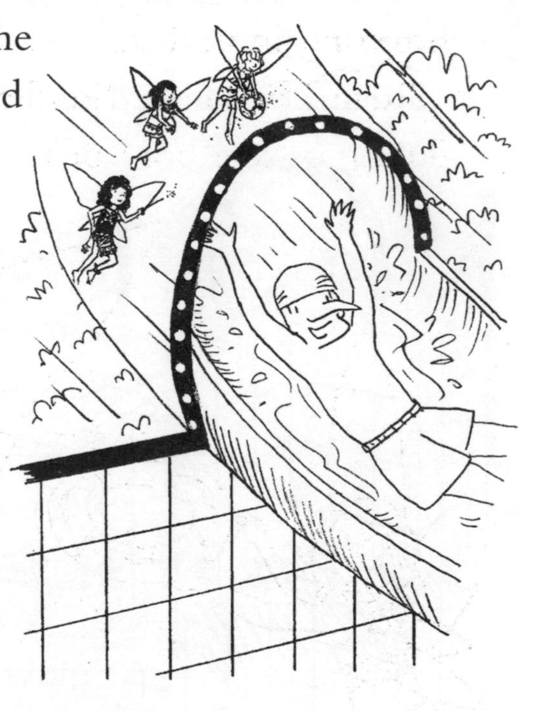

"There's our goblin," Kirsty said, spotting him as he lay on his tummy at the top of the slide. "But how are we going to track where he is when he's in the tube?" she asked. "It's going to be tricky to catch the right goblin if we don't know when our goggled-goblin's going to pop out."

Samantha winked and waved her wand. A stream of sparkles shot through the air towards the goblin as he pushed off into the tube.

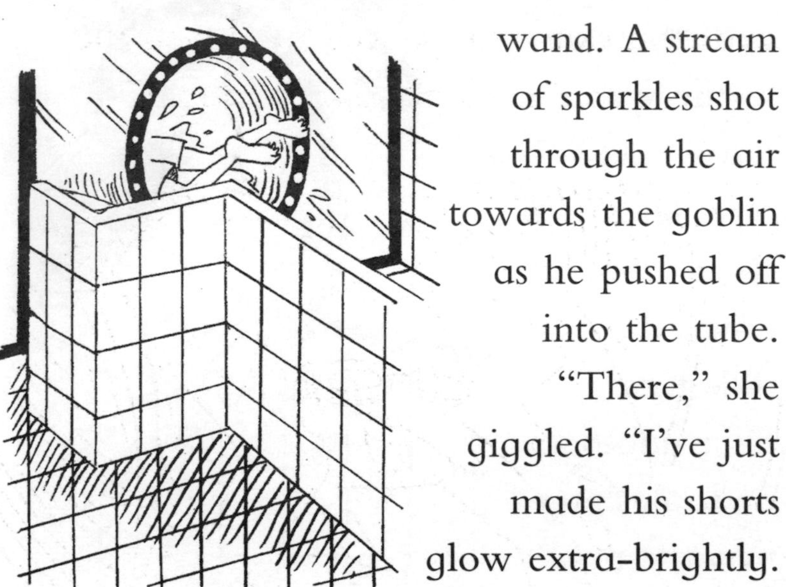

"There," she giggled. "I've just made his shorts glow extra-brightly.

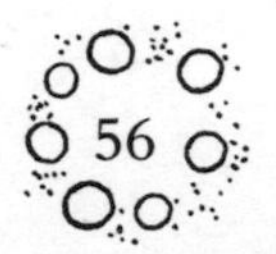

We should be able to see them shining through the slide, even when he's in the tube."

Rachel laughed. "There he is!" she cried, pointing to a twisty section of the slide where a bright blue glow shone through the tube.

"He's getting nearer," Kirsty said, as they saw the blue glow whizz round the bendy bit of pipe and approach the last section. "Let's get into position!"

Samantha waved her wand to make the rubber ring bigger. She and the girls were just preparing to lower it into the right spot, when they heard a cry go up from further down the pool.

"Hey, look out! Pesky fairies near the slide!"

Kirsty glanced over her shoulder and gulped. Several angry-looking goblins were pointing and swimming towards them.

She looked nervously at Rachel and Samantha. "We won't be able to catch the goblin on the slide if all the goblins come after us," she cried. "What are we going to do?"

Making Waves

"I'll take care of this," Samantha said, and pointed her wand at the water. A flurry of bubbles and sparkles streamed from the tip of her wand and into the pool. Immediately, huge waves appeared and began rolling towards the crowd of goblins as if a wave machine had been switched on.

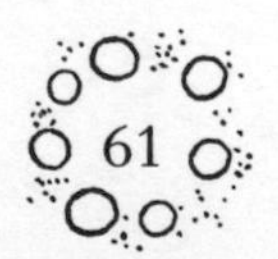

At first, the goblins tried to plough through the waves and reach the fairies, but then Samantha magicked up a load of bodyboards and water toys.

"Hey, I'm a super-surfer!" one goblin shouted, grabbing a board and riding a wave back to the shallow end. "Woohoo!"

All the goblins wanted to be super-surfers after that, some lying on boards and coasting along on the

waves, while others tried to jump up and stand. Soon they were all whooping with glee and playing in the waves, all thoughts of the fairies completely forgotten. Rachel and Kirsty couldn't help but chuckle.

"They won't bother us any more," Samantha said. "Now let's get the one with my goggles. Look, he's just about to come out of the chute!"

Sure enough, the goblin with the Magic Goggles was coming down the final run.

The three fairies gripped the rubber ring tightly.

"Here he comes!" Kirsty cried, and, a second later, the goblin with the Magic Goggles burst headfirst from the slide, straight into the rubber ring!

Thanks to Samantha's magic, the ring was just the right size to pin his arms to his sides, and when the girls let go, the goblin was left bobbing upright in the water like a big green cork.

Samantha flew over and tugged at the rubbery strap of her Magic Goggles. Kirsty and Rachel fluttered to help her.

"Hey!" shouted the goblin, scowling. "Those goggles are mine!"

"Oh, no, they're not," Samantha told him sternly. As the goggles came free, they shrank to their Fairyland size and

Samantha dangled them in front of his face. "Besides," she went on with a cheeky smile, "I don't think they would fit you now!"

Samantha touched her wand to the goggles and they sparkled even more brightly for a moment. Kirsty and Rachel knew that now the Magic Goggles were back with Samantha, their powers would start working again, and swimming would be fun and safe in the human world and throughout Fairyland.

"Hurrah!" Rachel cheered happily,

as she, Samantha and Kirsty zoomed safely up and out of the goblin's reach. Then Samantha put on her Magic Goggles and used her magic to calm the waves and lift the ring off the goblin, setting him free. He splashed off miserably to join his friends.

The lifeguard, seeing what had happened, shouted grumpily, "Everyone out of the pool. It's time to go back to Jack Frost's castle."

All the goblins clambered reluctantly out of the pool, collected their towels and clothes, and marched off. It was very quiet once they'd gone.

"What a mess!" Kirsty said, gazing down at all the floats, rings and bodyboards still bobbing about in the water.

"This won't take long to clear up," Samantha promised, and waved her wand again. In a swirl of light pink fairy dust, the floats and toys rose up out of the water and put themselves tidily away, the rubber rings rolling into the cupboard like big colourful wheels.

Once the pool was back to normal, the three friends flew out through the open window, and Samantha used her magic to turn Kirsty and Rachel back into girls wearing outdoor clothes once more.

"I'd better go to Fairyland, to make sure everything's ready for the swimming events in the Fairyland Olympics," Samantha said, kissing Rachel and Kirsty goodbye. "Thank you so much for your help. Where are you going now?"

"We need to catch a bus to Aqua World," Rachel said.

Samantha nodded and waved her wand in a complicated pattern. A pink glittery ticket appeared in each girl's hand. "This'll be quicker," Samantha said.

"When you're ready, just touch the tickets together. They're full of special fairy dust, and will take you straight to Aqua World."

"Oh, thank you!" Kirsty cried, looking at her ticket in delight. What an exciting day this was turning out to be.

The girls said goodbye to Samantha and watched as she flew off into the distance.

"That was fun," Rachel said, holding her ticket out towards Kirsty's. "And I'm really looking forward to doing some swimming myself, now."

"Me too," Kirsty agreed, touching her ticket to Rachel's and feeling herself getting swept up by fairy magic. "But not as much as I'm looking forward to how we get there!"

Now Kirsty and Rachel must help...

Alice the Tennis Fairy

Read on for a sneak peek...

"Isn't it a gorgeous day, Kirsty?" said Rachel Walker happily. She and her best friend, Kirsty Tate, were walking along a country path not far from the Walkers' house, enjoying the sunshine. "And it would be even better if we could find another Magic Sporty Object!"

"Yes!" Kirsty agreed. "It's only two more days until the Fairy Olympics, and Alice the Tennis Fairy's Magic Racquet and Gemma the Gymnastics Fairy's Magic Hoop are still missing."

Rachel and Kirsty had promised to help their friends, the Sporty Fairies, find their seven Magic Sporty Objects. Sports in both the human and the fairy worlds were being disrupted because these objects had been stolen by Jack Frost and his goblin servants.

Jack Frost was determined that his goblin team would win the Fairy Olympics and the cup filled with good luck.

He knew that the power of the Magic Sporty Objects meant that anyone close to one of them immediately became brilliant at that particular sport, so he had sent his goblins into the human world with each object, and told them to practise for the fairy games.

As the girls walked on down the lane, Rachel suddenly noticed a strange sign pinned to a tree. "Look at that sign," she remarked, pointing it out to Kirsty.

The words on the sign had been painted very messily in bright green paint. "'Goblindon'," Kirsty read aloud. "And there's an arrow with the words 'Entrance to Tippington Tennis Club - this way' written underneath it," she added.

"Oh, no!" Rachel exclaimed. "This has got goblin mischief written all over it! Mum and I have played tennis at the club once or twice and there are always lots of people around. What if the goblins have been spotted by someone?"

Kirsty looked worried. The girls knew that nobody in the human world was supposed to find out about Fairyland and its inhabitants.

"We must find out what's going on," Kirsty said urgently. "If the goblins are at the tennis club, they might have Alice's Magic Racquet..."

"Good thinking," Rachel agreed.

As the girls hurried off towards the tennis club entrance, they suddenly heard a loud voice coming from behind the hedge.

"Attention, goblins!" the voice announced. "I shall now explain the rules of the tournament."

"The goblins are having a tennis tournament!" Rachel exclaimed. "Instead of Wimbledon, it's Goblindon!"

"There's only one rule," the goblin went on. "I'm the umpire in charge of this tournament, so what I say, goes!"

He chuckled loudly, but Rachel and Kirsty could hear the sound of other goblins muttering and complaining.

"How many of them *are* there?" Kirsty asked with a frown...

Read Alice the Tennis Fairy to find out what adventures are in store for Kirsty and Rachel!

Meet the Sporty Fairies

Join Rachel and Kirsty as they help the Sporty Fairies to foil Jack Frost's naughty plot to mess up the Fairyland Olympics!

www.rainbowmagicbooks.co.uk

Win Rainbow Magic Goodies!

There are lots of Rainbow Magic fairies, and we want to know which one is your favourite! Send us a picture of her and tell us in thirty words why she is your favourite and why you like Rainbow Magic books. Each month we will put the entries into a draw and select one winner to receive a Rainbow Magic Sparkly T-shirt and Goody Bag!

Send your entry on a postcard to Rainbow Magic Competition, Orchard Books, 338 Euston Road, London NW1 3BH.
Australian readers should email: childrens.books@hachette.com.au
New Zealand readers should write to Rainbow Magic Competition, 4 Whetu Place, Mairangi Bay, Auckland NZ.
Don't forget to include your name and address.
Only one entry per child.

Good luck!

Meet the Music Fairies

Jack Frost has stolen the Music Fairies' magical notes! Kirsty and Rachel must get them back or music will never sound sweet again.

www.rainbowmagicbooks.co.uk